P9-CQB-523

TM

A Day in the Country

An Alphabet Story

By Liza Alexander
Illustrated by Rick Wetzel

Featuring Jim Henson's Sesame Street Muppets

A Sesame Street / Golden Press Book
Published by Western Publishing Company, Inc.,
in conjunction with Children's Television Workshop.

© 1988 Children's Television Workshop. Sesame Street Muppets © Muppets, Inc. 1988. All rights reserved. Printed in the U.S.A. No part of this book may be reproduced or copied in any form without written permission from the publisher. Sesame Street®, the Sesame Street sign, and Sesame Street GET READY are trademarks and service marks of Children's Television Workshop. GOLDEN®, GOLDEN & DESIGN®, GOLDEN PRESS®, and A GOLDEN BOOK® are trademarks of Western Publishing Company, Inc. Library of Congress Catalog Card Number: 87-81932 ISBN: 0-307-13106-8 / ISBN: 0-307-63106-0 (lib. bdg.)
C D E F G H I J K L M

The Sesame Street gang was all set to go to the country for the day and stopped to say good-bye to Big Bird. He had a cold and had to stay home.

"We will miss you very much, Big Bird!" said Grover. "Get better, and we will see you soon!"

As soon as they got off the bus Bert said, "All right, everybody, let's play a groovy game. Let's each find things that begin with letters of the alphabet. I'll go first and find things that begin with the letter A.

"Let's see..." He looked around.

"Aha! An angry army of ants ambling over an apple. And an airplane flying across the azure sky."

"Awesome!" added Ernie.

Bb

"Boy, old buddy Bert," said Ernie, "I'll begin with the letter B."

He went searching through the woods and saw a baby bear and a beehive beneath a beautiful blossoming tree.

Cc

"Cowabunga!" said Cookie Monster. He chose the letter C. He carried a carton of chocolate chip cookies and came across country things to chomp on—chewy cherries and chestnuts, and crunchy carrots and corn.

"I'll do the letter D," said Prairie Dawn. She dashed off to discover a dog digging up dirt. A deer darted over some daffodils, and a duck looked dizzy.

Elmo was eagerly on the E trail. An eagle sat in an elegant evergreen tree. “All you have to do is use your ears and eyes,” explained Elmo, picking eggplants.

Ff

Grover saw a frog floating on a pond not far from the forest.

In a grassy glade Grover wore gloves and gathered grapes. He gave them to a gabby goose and a gray goat.

"Gee!" said Grover. "You guys were hungry."

Hh

Elmo hiked up a high hill. Some Honkers were hopping over hay bales.

"Honk, honk!" honked the Honkers in hats.

"Howdy!" Elmo hollered.

Ii

Prairie Dawn thought the flavors at the Ice Cream Igloo were icky and that too much ice cream would make her ill.

Jj

Instead, she just ate a jarful of jelly beans and some jam, took off her jazzy jacket, and had a jolly time jumping rope.

Kk

Bert tracked the letter K. He blew kisses to two kindly kittens and played them a tune on his kazoo.

Ll

Cookie Monster liked to look for things that began with the letter L. "How lucky!" he said with a laugh when he saw a lively little lamb leap over a line of lovely lemons, lettuces, and limes.

Mm

Ernie marched off with a map to find the letter M. He marveled at a mouse and a mighty moose who munched upon a mound of moss.

Nn

As Elmo nibbled on nuts he noticed that he was near a nice nest. “Nifty!” said Elmo. “Nine noisy birds!”

Oo

In a barnyard Oscar howled at an old owl who sat on the branch of an orange tree.

Pp

Some pigs pranced and plunged into a pile of potato peels, pears, peaches, prunes, pumpkins, and pineapples.

Qq

A duck quacked as she quarreled with a quail over a quilt.

Rr

Rubber Duckie, a raccoon, and a rooster romped on a raft in a river. Under a rainbow they rocked to the music on a radio.

"This is super!" said Grover. "I see so many animals whose names begin with the letter S. I spy a splashing swan, a sleeping squirrel, and a spooky spider.

"Sensational!"

Tt

Cookie Monster took tea beneath a tall tree with two turtles and a twiddlebug. They tasted tough toast, tiny tomatoes, and ten tacos.

“Unbelievable!” said Bert. “It’s starting to rain.” He unfolded his umbrella and got under it.

Elmo picked violets to put in a vase. “This is a very fine valentine for my mommy,” he said.

Ernie, Bert, and Cookie Monster watched a worm wiggle over a watermelon in a wheelbarrow.

Grover played a xylophone.

"Yes!" yelled Oscar. "I love that yucchy sound."
Then Oscar did a trick with his yo-yo.

Prairie Dawn helped Elmo zip up his zipper.
It was time to go home.

It had been an exciting day in the country. Back on Sesame Street the first thing the gang did was go and see Big Bird. He felt much better.

"We played an alphabet game in the country," said Bert.

"Look, Big Bird," said Grover. "We brought you a present for every letter of the alphabet."

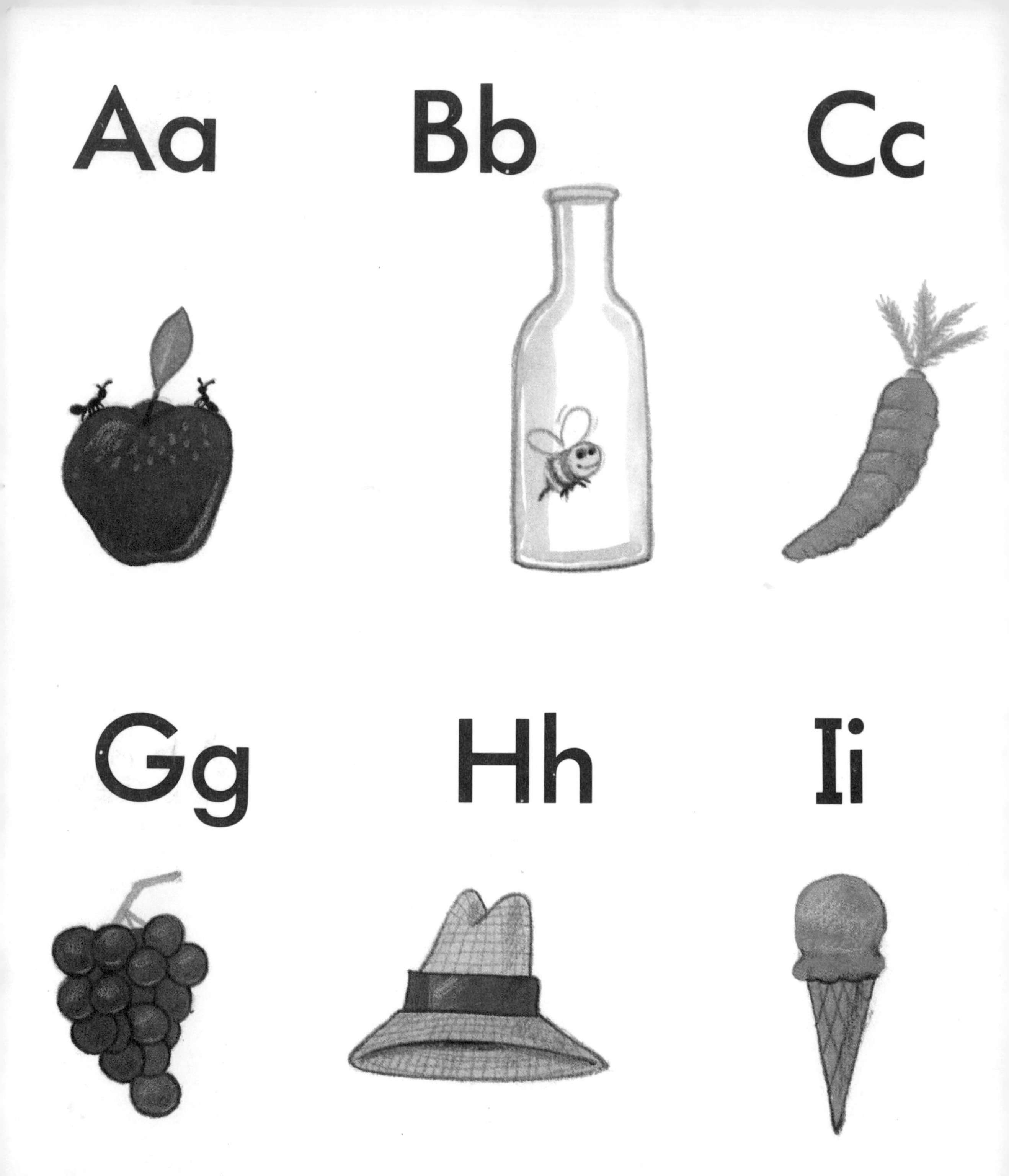
Aa
Bb
Cc
Gg
Hh
Ii

Dd
Ee
Ff
Jj
Kk
Ll
Mm

Nn Oo Pp Qq
Uu Vv Ww

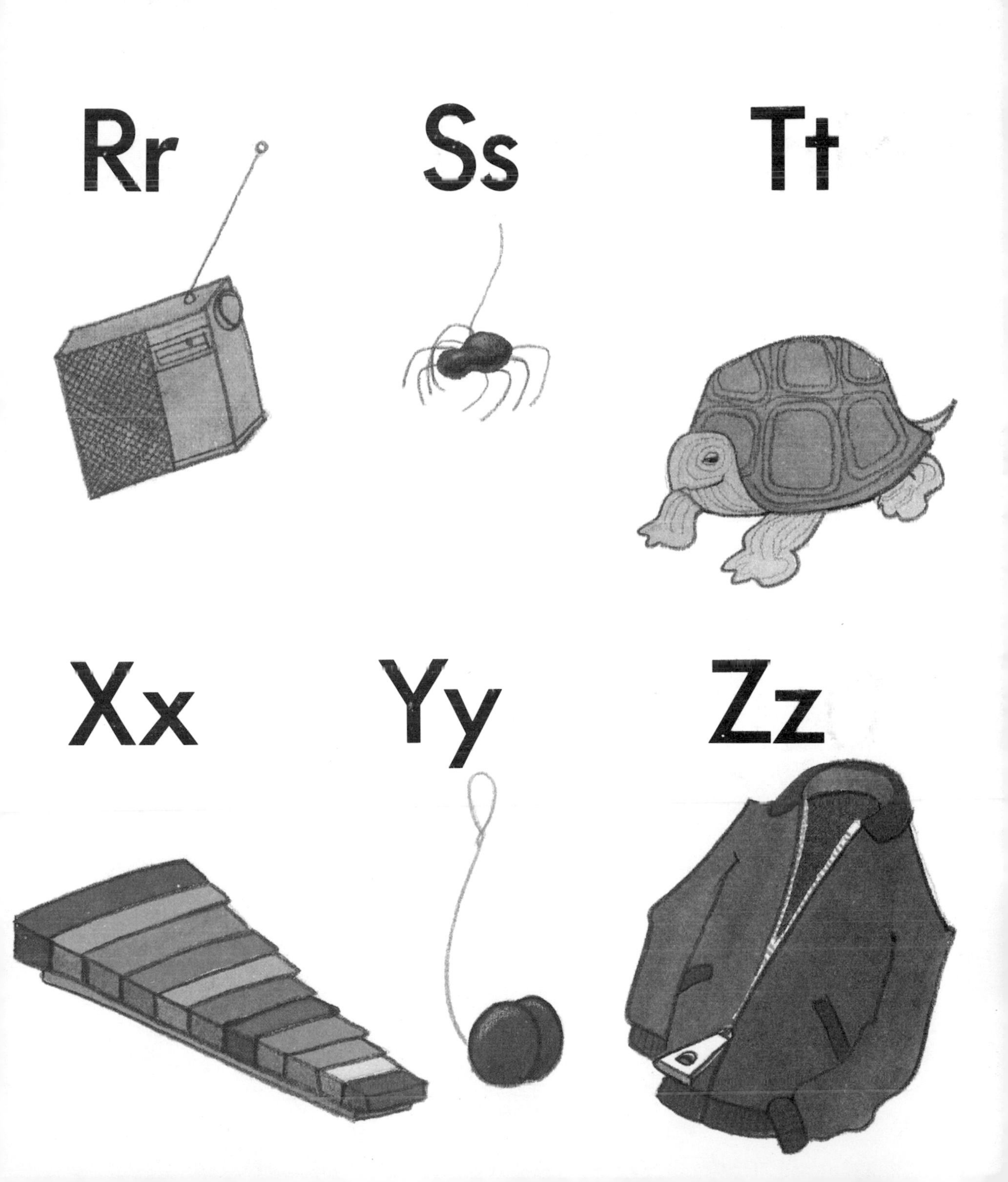
Rr
Ss
Tt
Xx
Yy
Zz

"Thank you, everybody! These presents make me feel like I spent the day in the country after all!" said Big Bird. "And now I know my alphabet, too!"